W9-CFQ-563

THE EVIL SWARM

BY DAVID ORME

STONE ARCH BOOKS
www.stonearchbooks.com

Library of Congress Cataloging-in-Publication Data
Orme, David, 1948 Mar. 1–
   [Boffin Boy and the Deadly Swarm]
   The Evil Swarm / by David Orme; illustrated by Peter Richardson.
   p. cm. — (Billy Blaster)
   Originally published: Boffin Boy and the Deadly Swarm. Watlington: Ransom, 2007.
   ISBN 978-1-4342-1274-0 (library binding)
   1. Graphic novels. [1. Graphic novels. 2. Heroes—Fiction. 3. Science fiction.]
I. Richardson, Peter, 1965– ill. II. Title.
PZ7.7.O76Evi 2009
741.5'941—dc22   2008031287

Summary:
A swarm of angry insects emerges from a volcano and attacks the people of Zone City.
With help from his super hero friends, Billy Blaster braves the depths of the volcano to
find the secret of the giant bugs. Billy has to think fast — danger is around every corner.
Billy and his friends must outsmart the evil swarm, or the whole planet is doomed!

Creative Director: Heather Kindseth
Graphic Designer: Carla Zetina-Yglesias

1 2 3 4 5 6 14 13 12 11 10 09

Printed in the United States of America

BILLY BLASTER

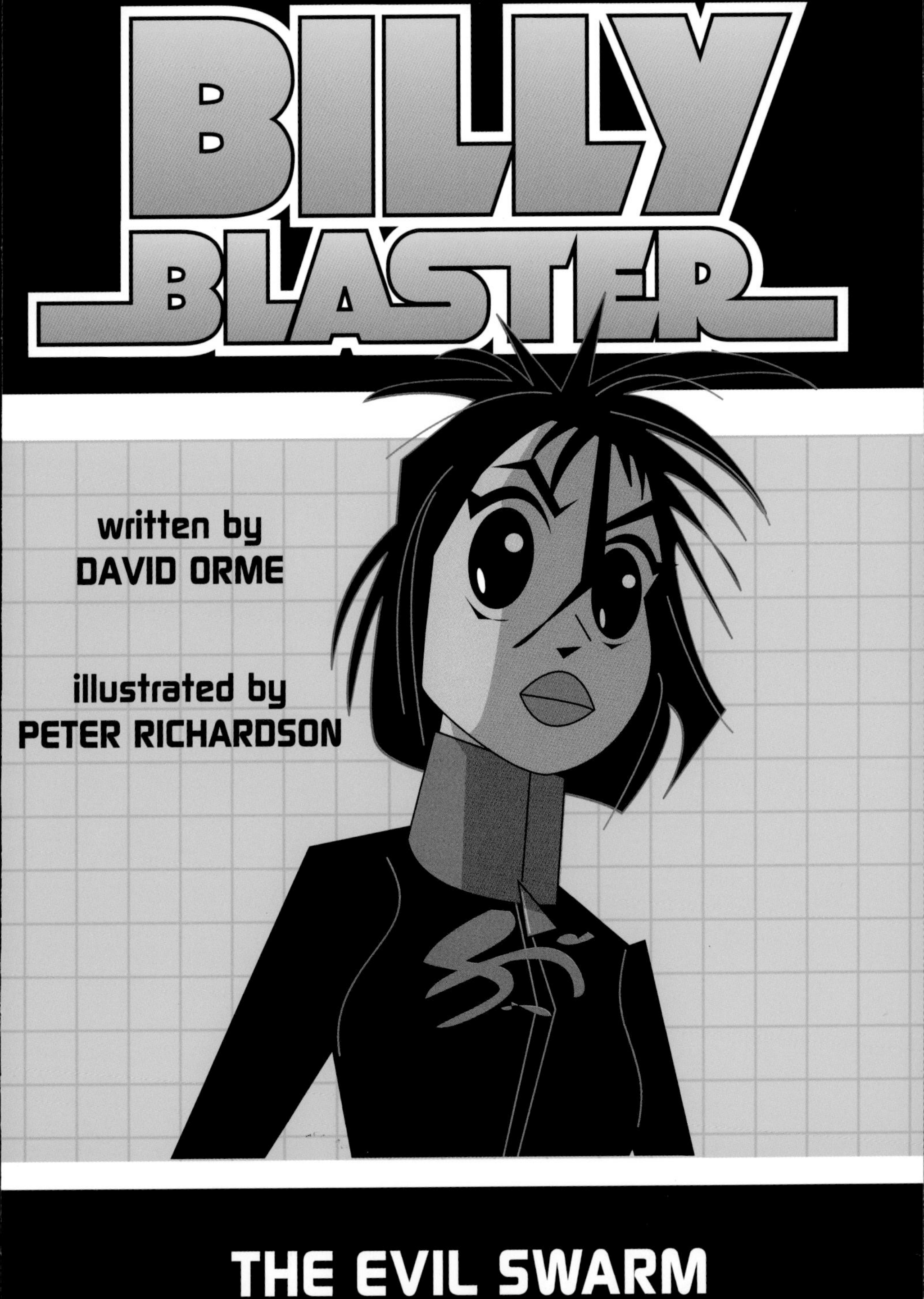

written by
DAVID ORME

illustrated by
PETER RICHARDSON

THE EVIL SWARM

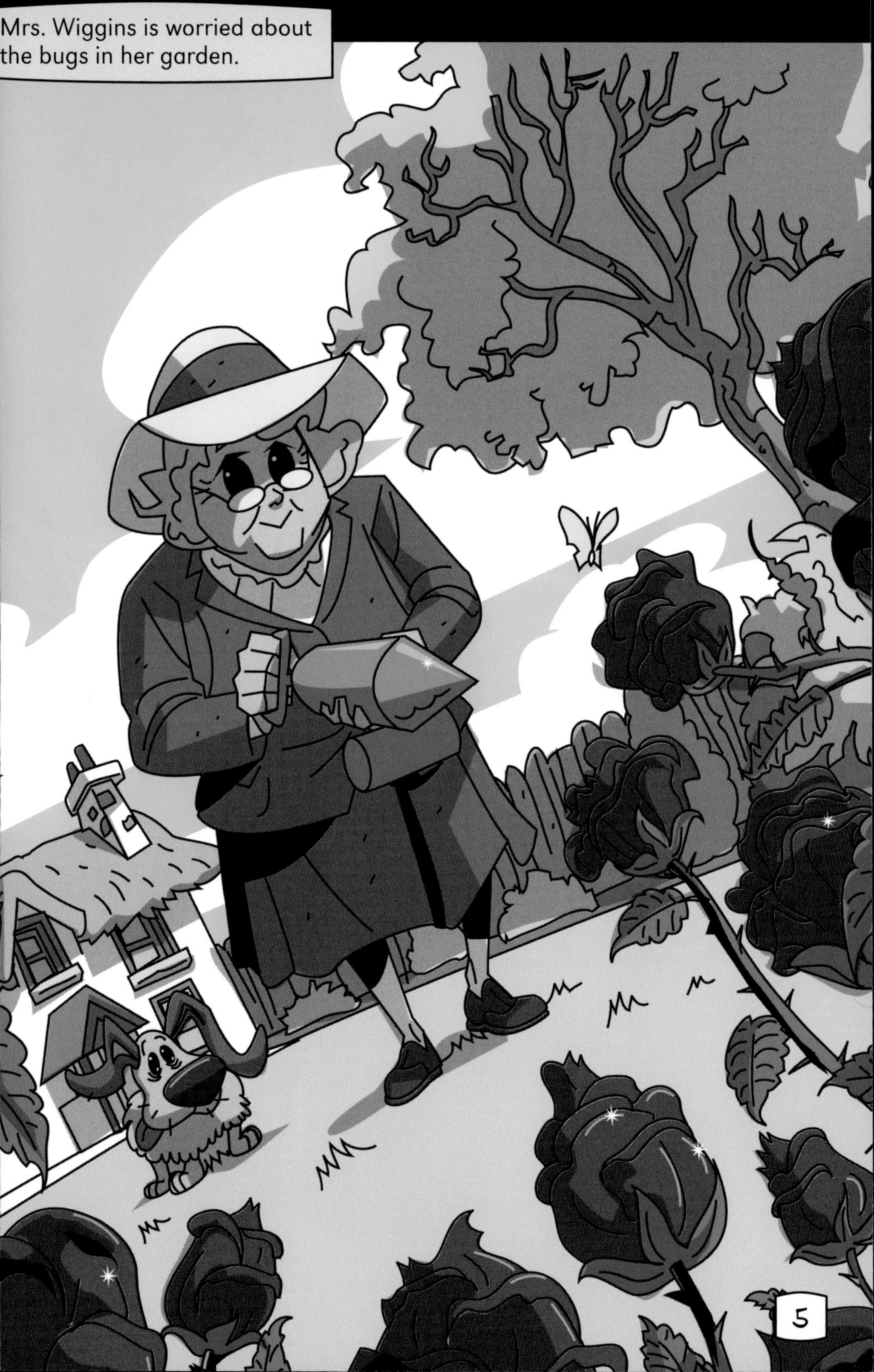
Mrs. Wiggins is worried about the bugs in her garden.

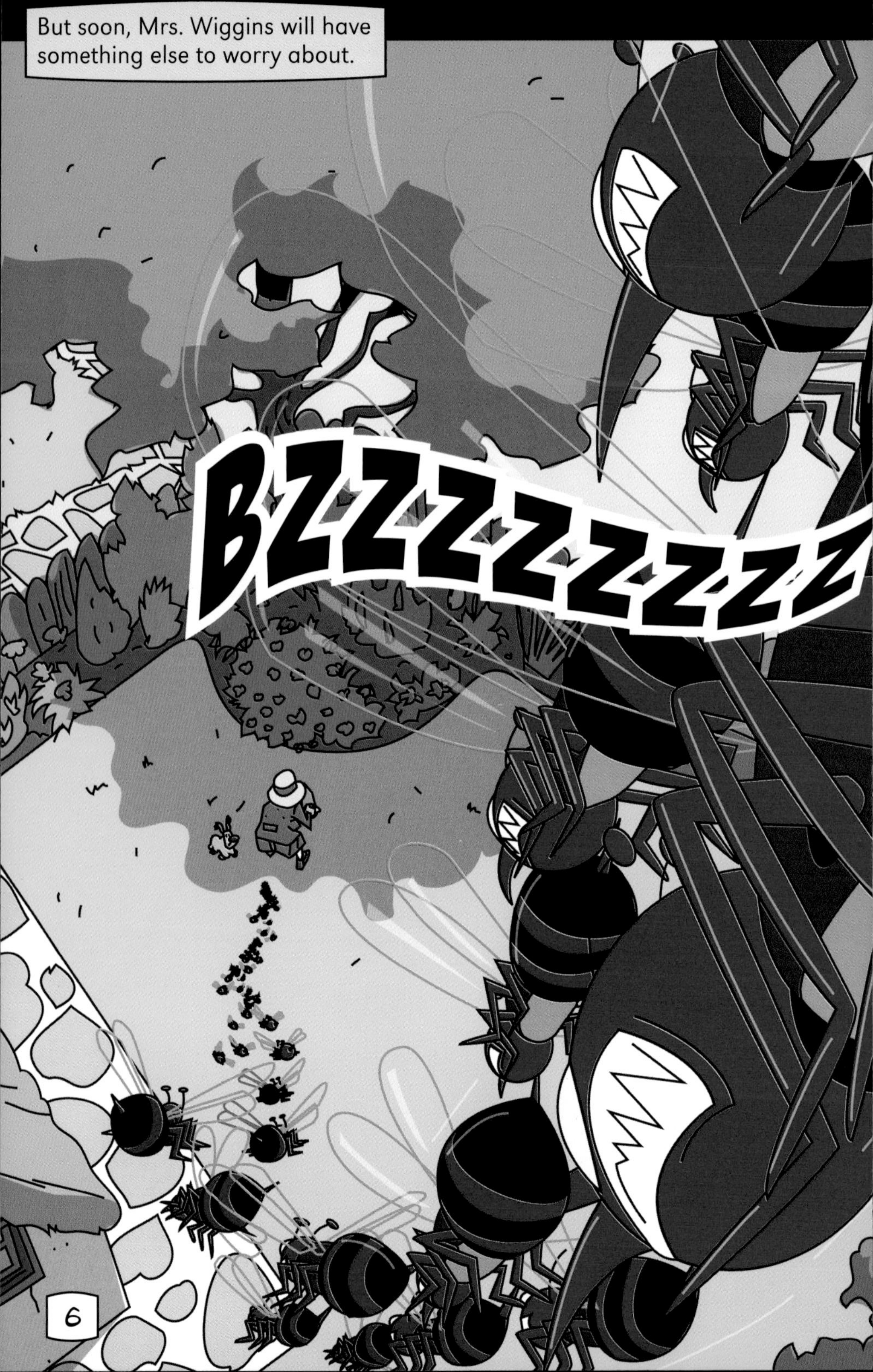
But soon, Mrs. Wiggins will have something else to worry about.
BZZZZZZZZ

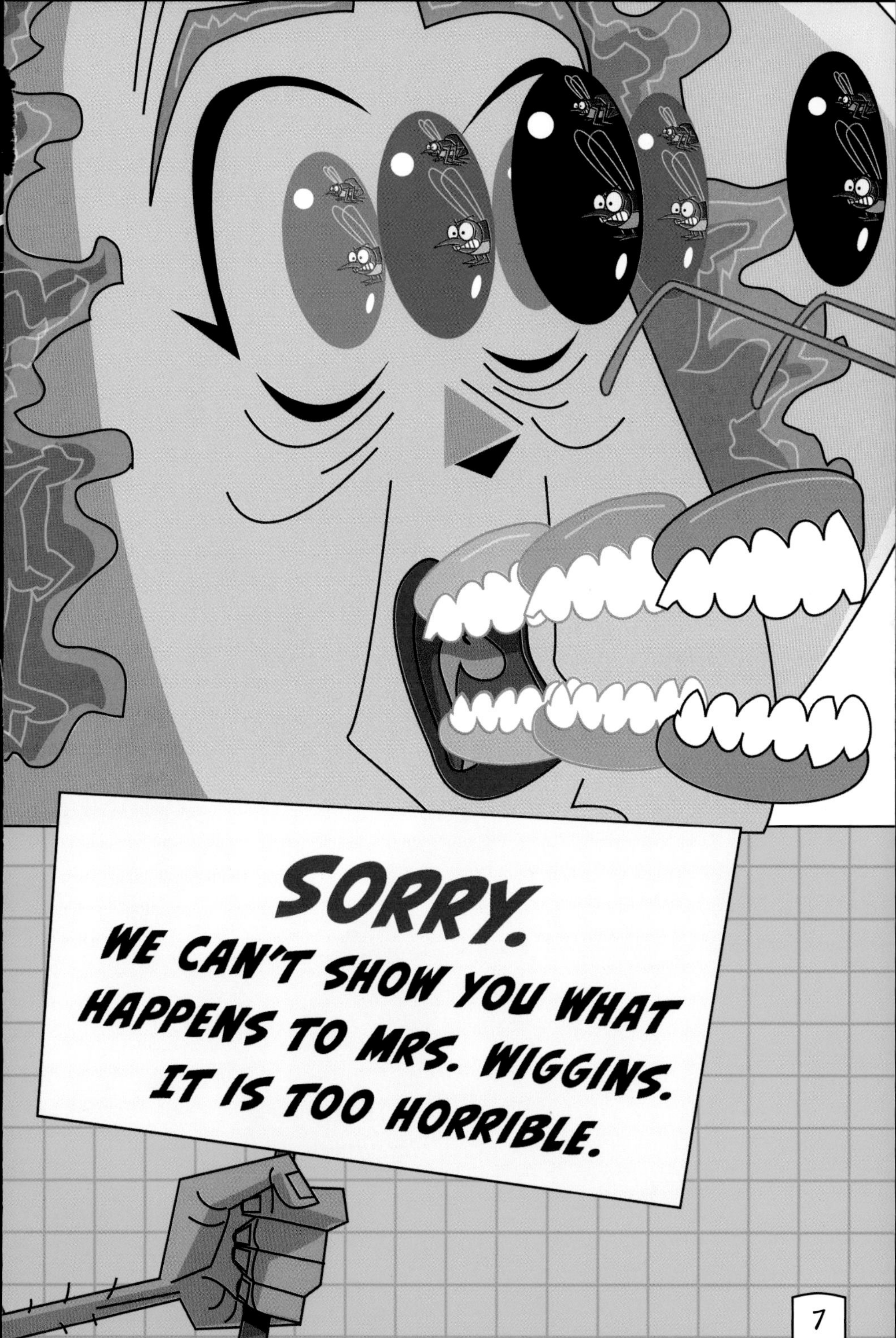
SORRY.
WE CAN'T SHOW YOU WHAT HAPPENS TO MRS. WIGGINS. IT IS TOO HORRIBLE.

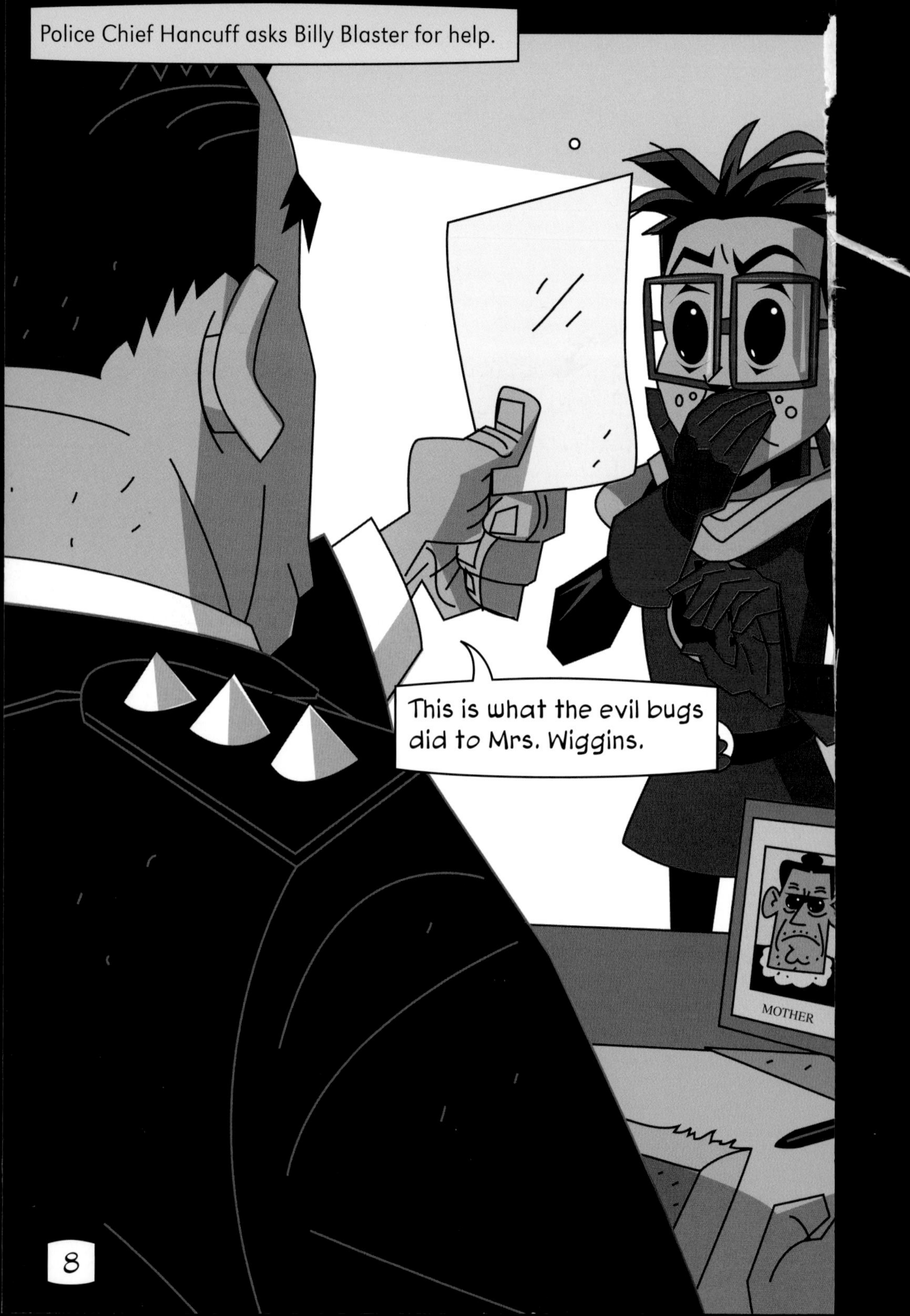
Police Chief Hancuff asks Billy Blaster for help.
This is what the evil bugs did to Mrs. Wiggins.
MOTHER

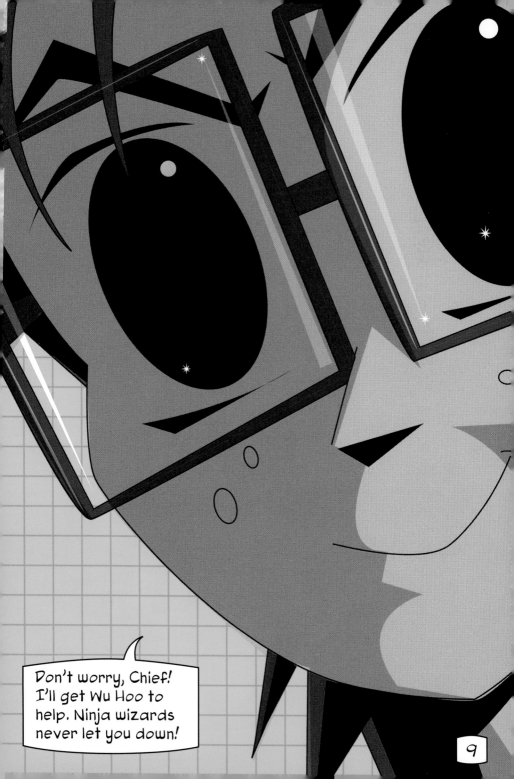

Don't worry, Chief!
I'll get Wu Hoo to
help. Ninja wizards
never let you down!

9

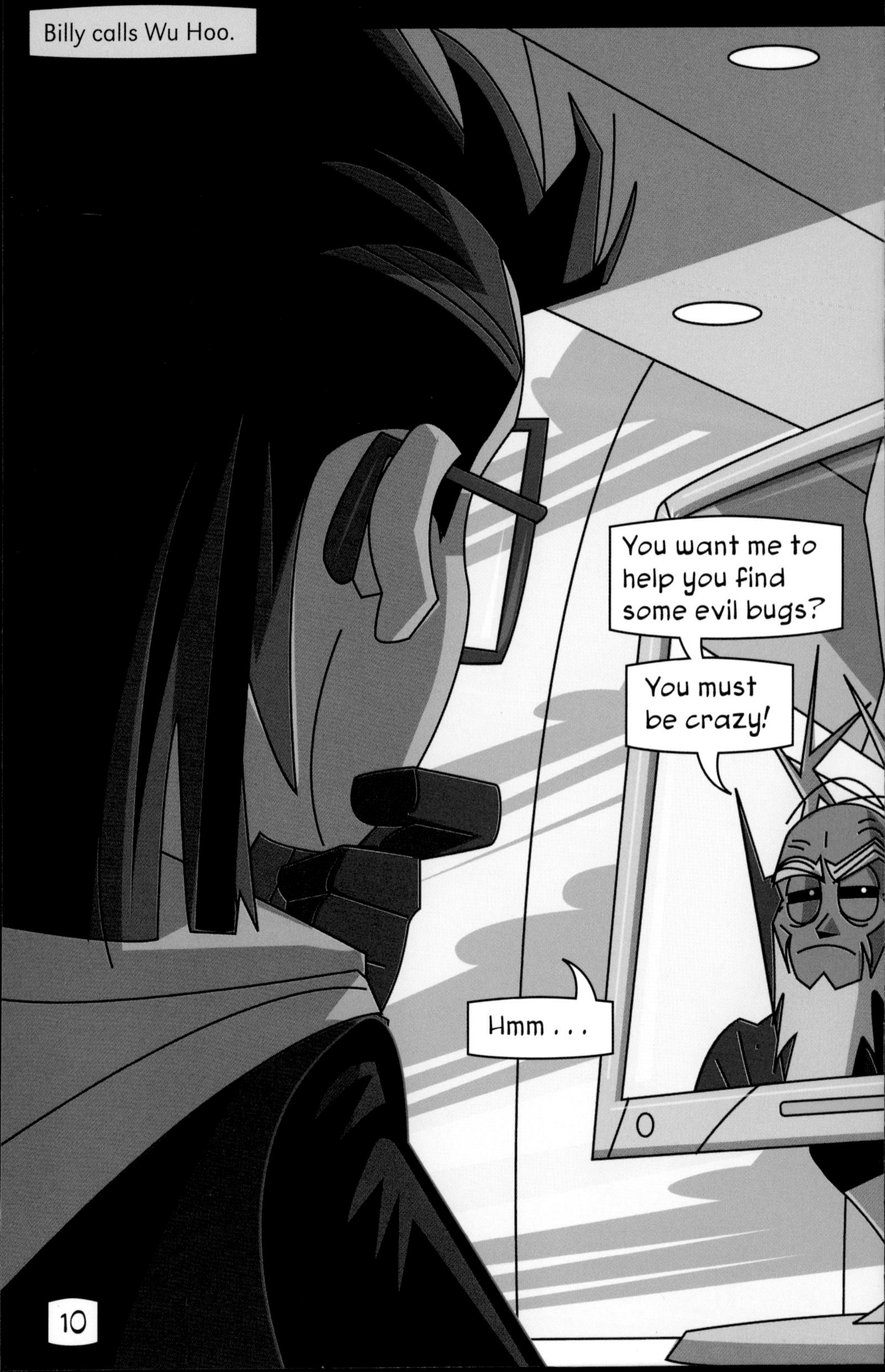
Billy calls Wu Hoo.
You want me to help you find some evil bugs?
You must be crazy!
Hmm . . .

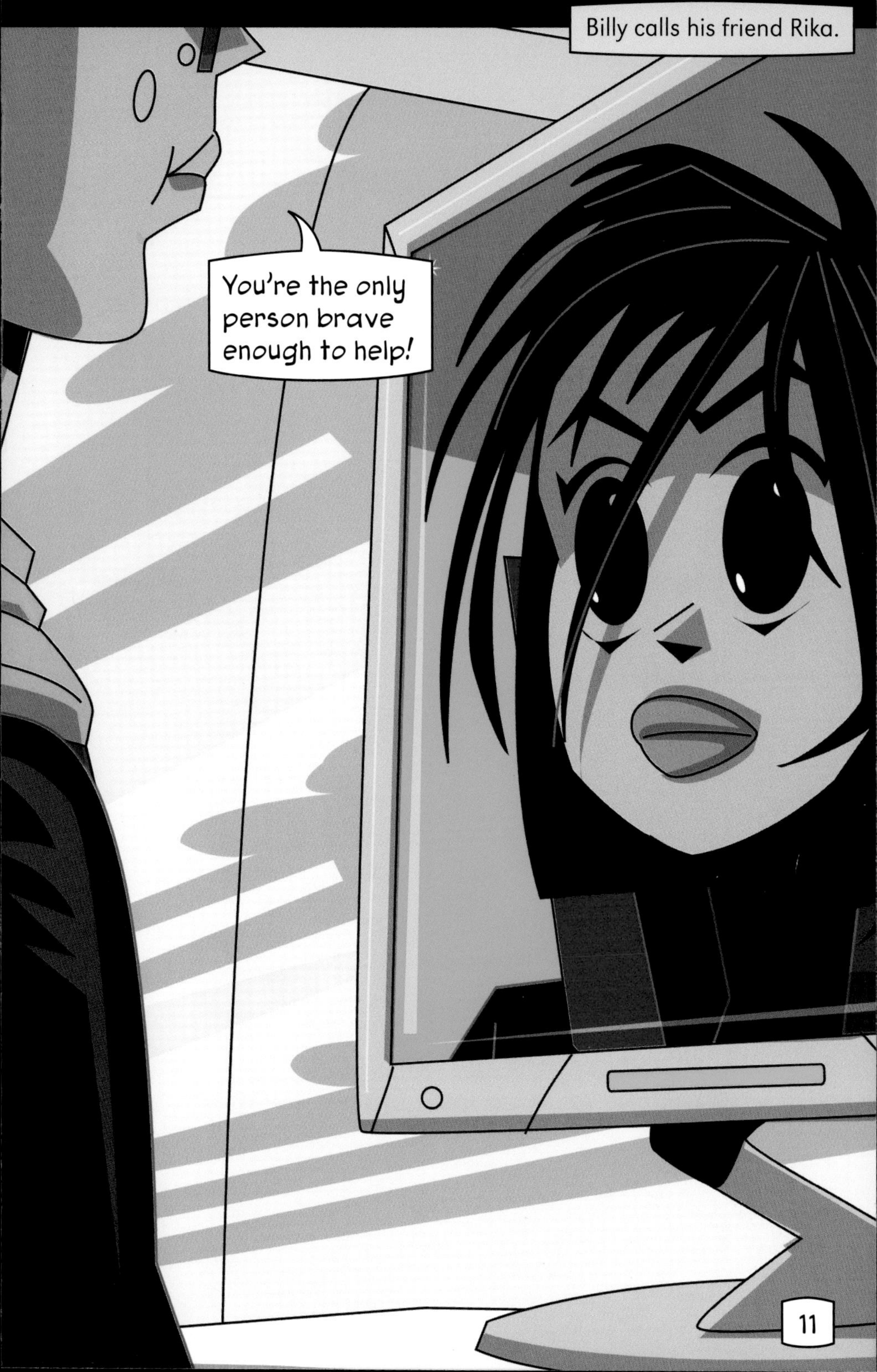
Billy calls his friend Rika.
You're the only person brave enough to help!

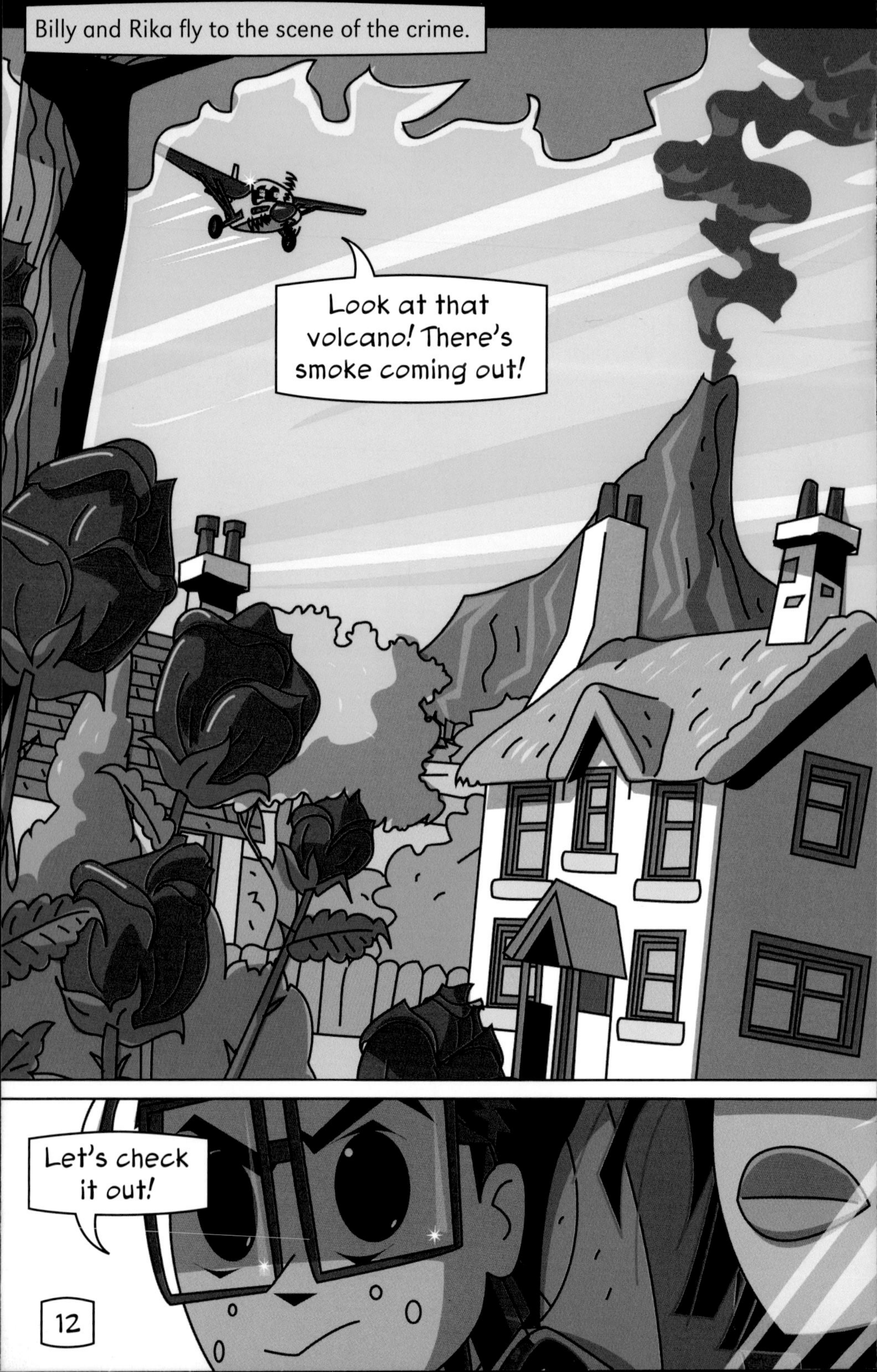
Billy and Rika fly to the scene of the crime.
Look at that volcano! There's smoke coming out!
Let's check it out!

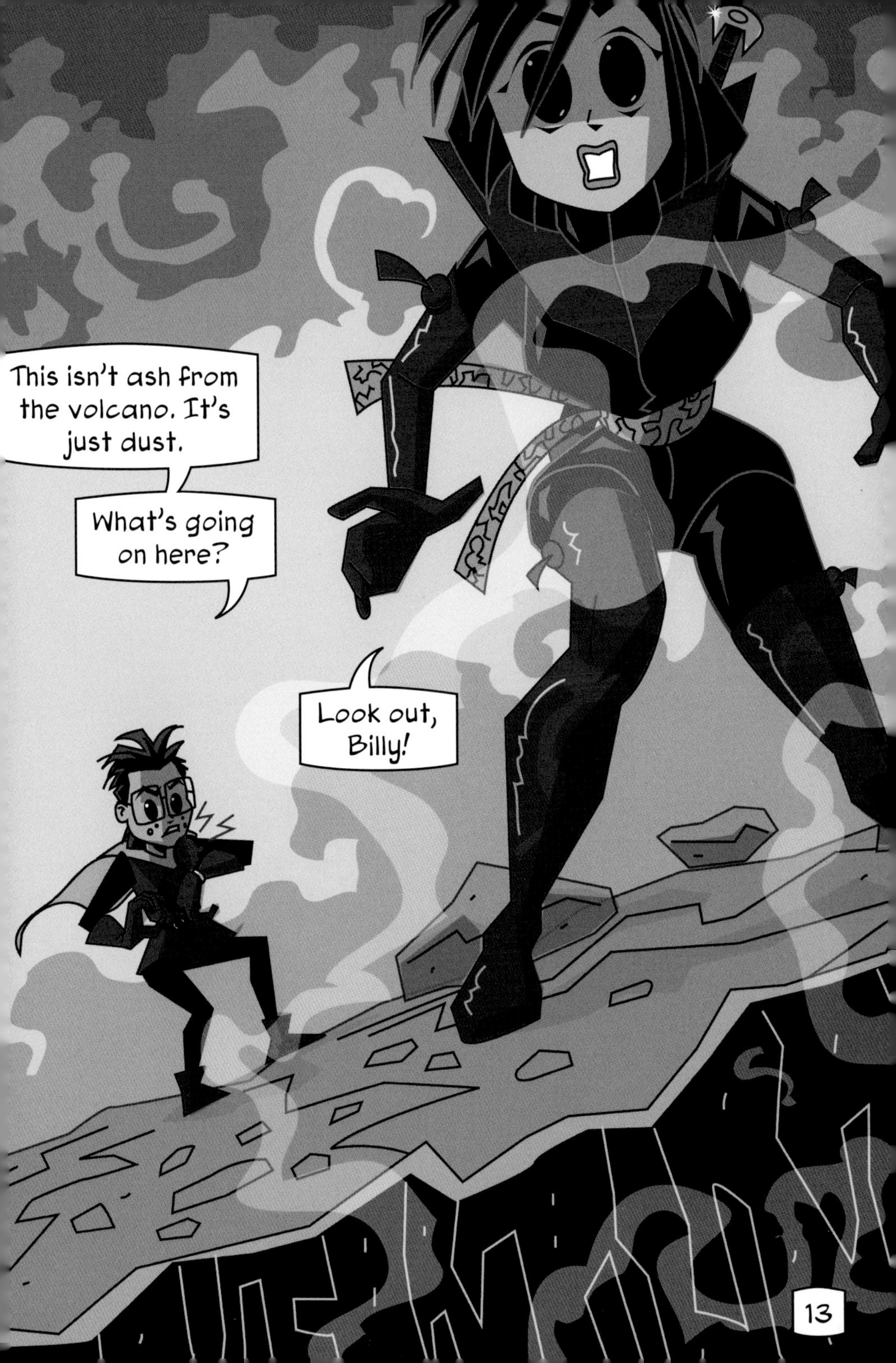
This isn't ash from the volcano. It's just dust.
What's going on here?
Look out, Billy!

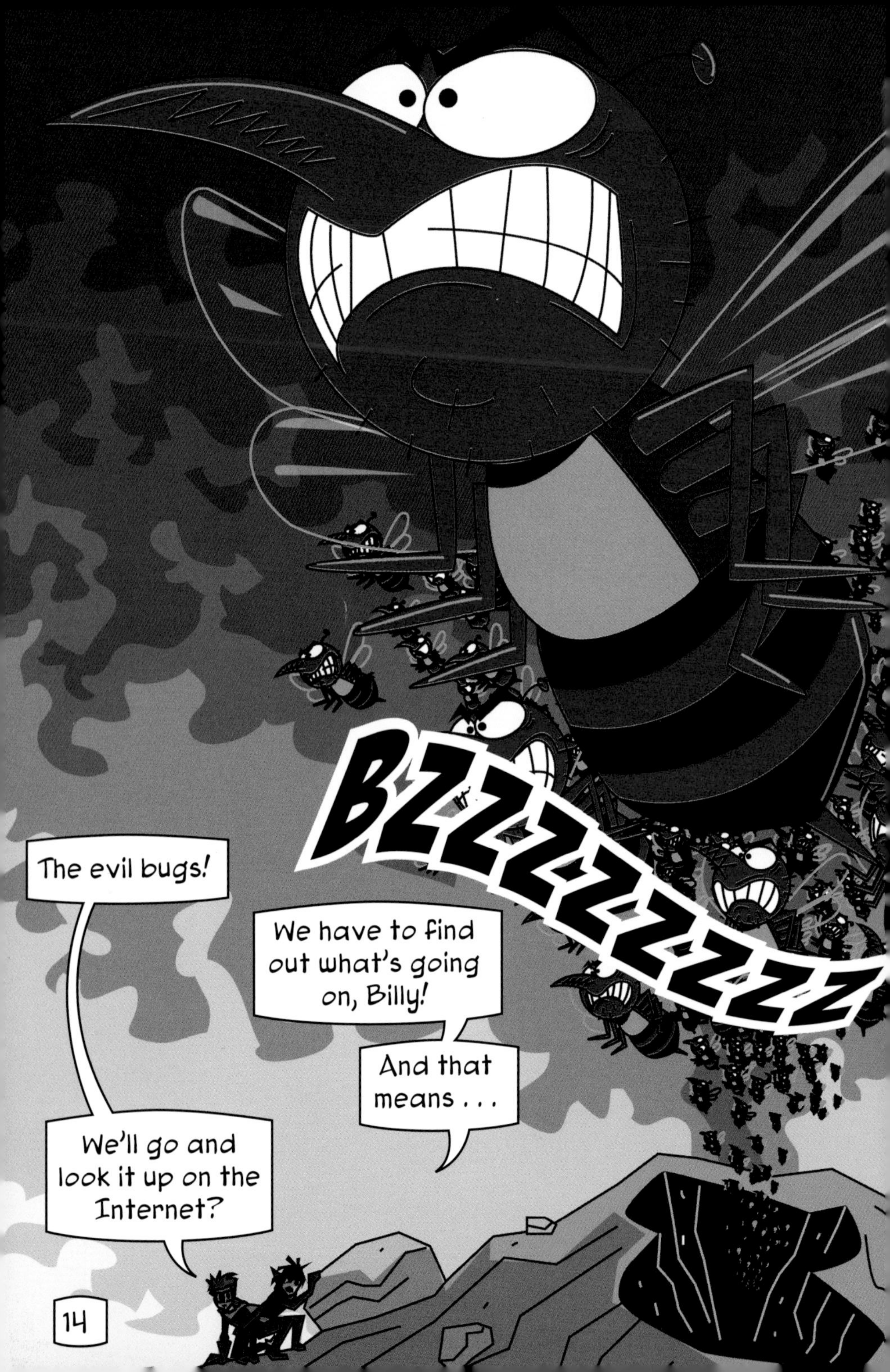
BZZZZZZZZZZ
The evil bugs!
We have to find out what's going on, Billy!
And that means . . .
We'll go and look it up on the Internet?

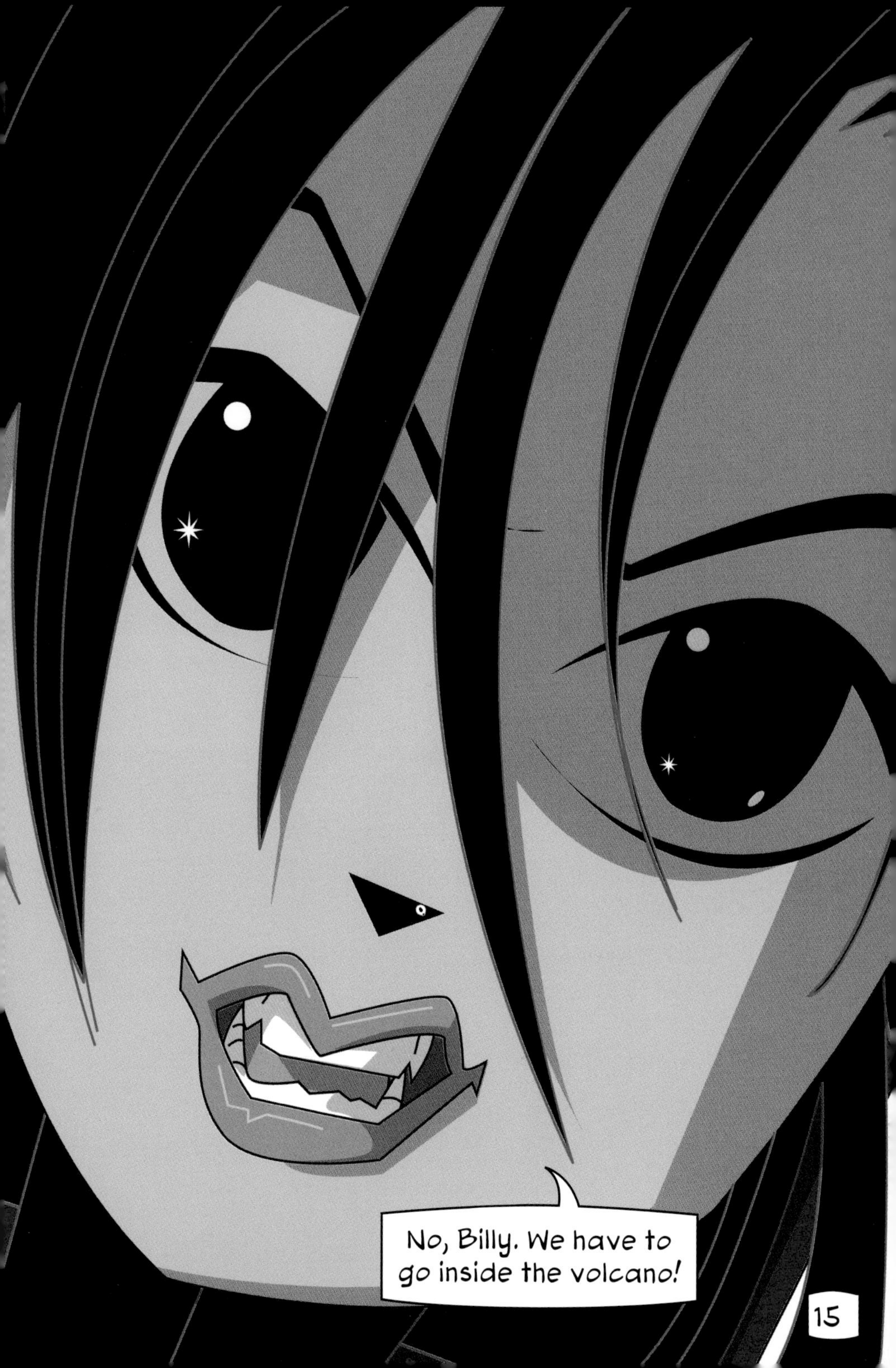
No, Billy. We have to go inside the volcano!

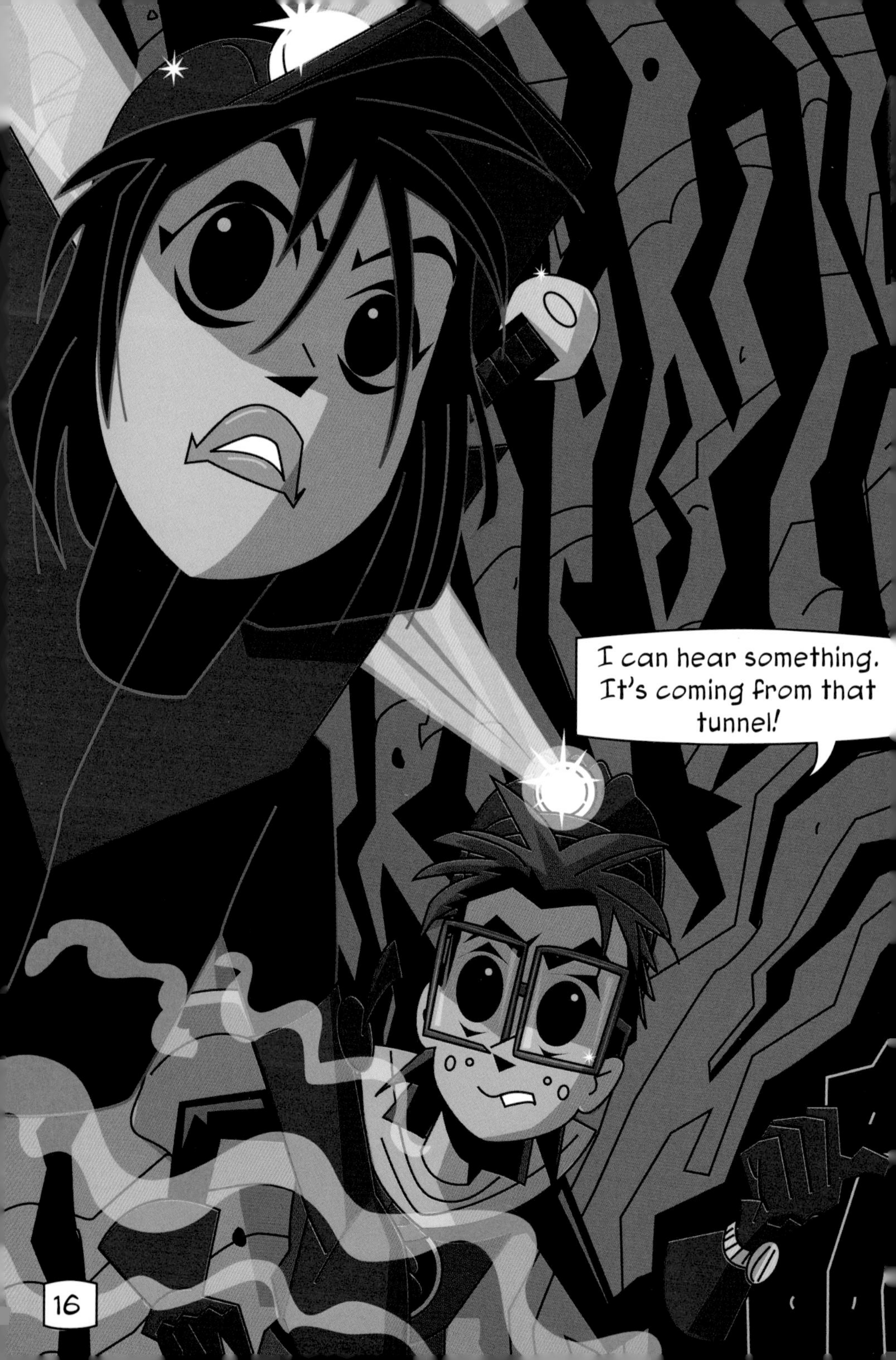
I can hear something. It's coming from that tunnel!

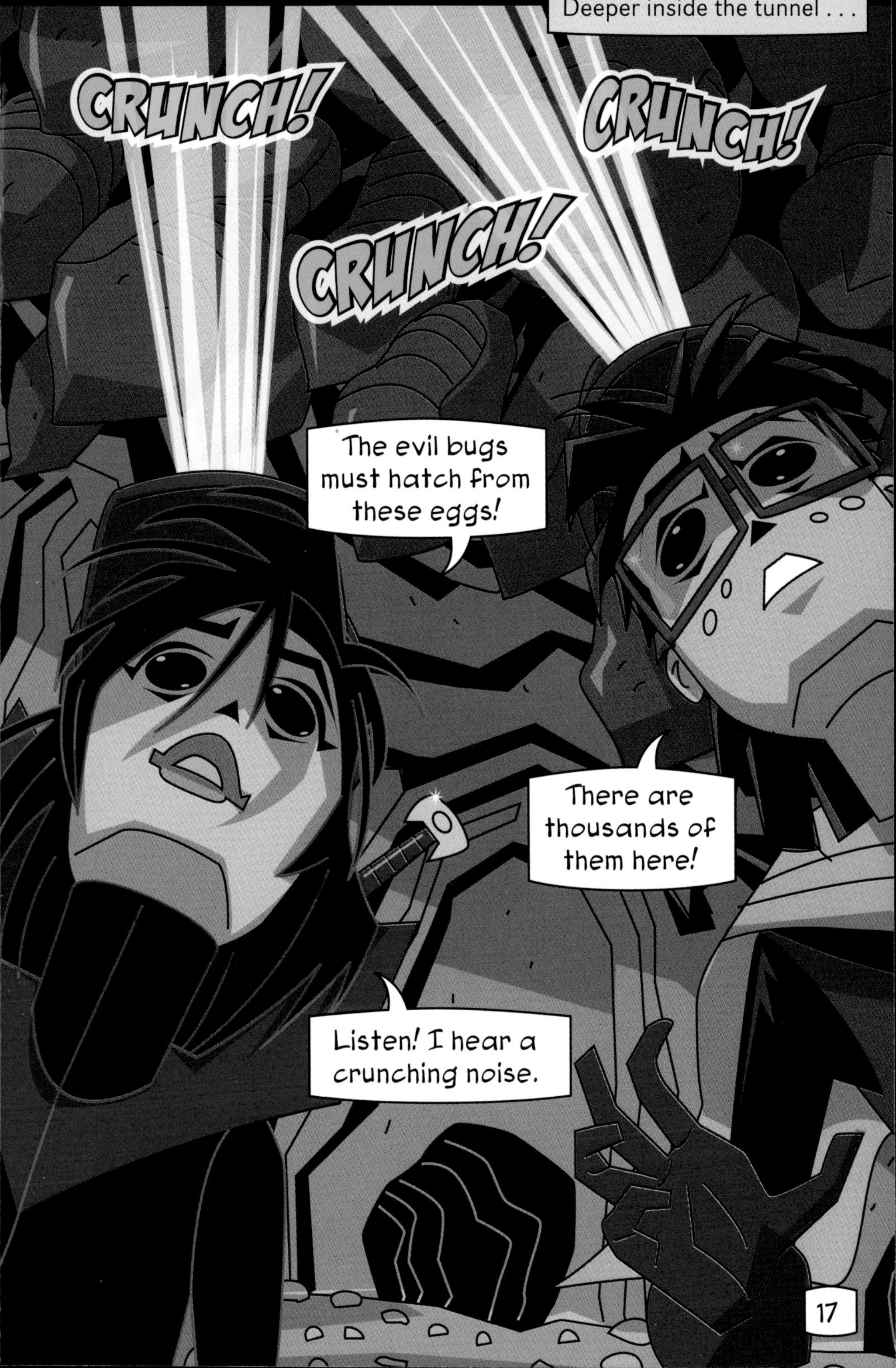
Deeper inside the tunnel . . .
CRUNCH!
CRUNCH!
CRUNCH!
The evil bugs must hatch from these eggs!
There are thousands of them here!
Listen! I hear a crunching noise.

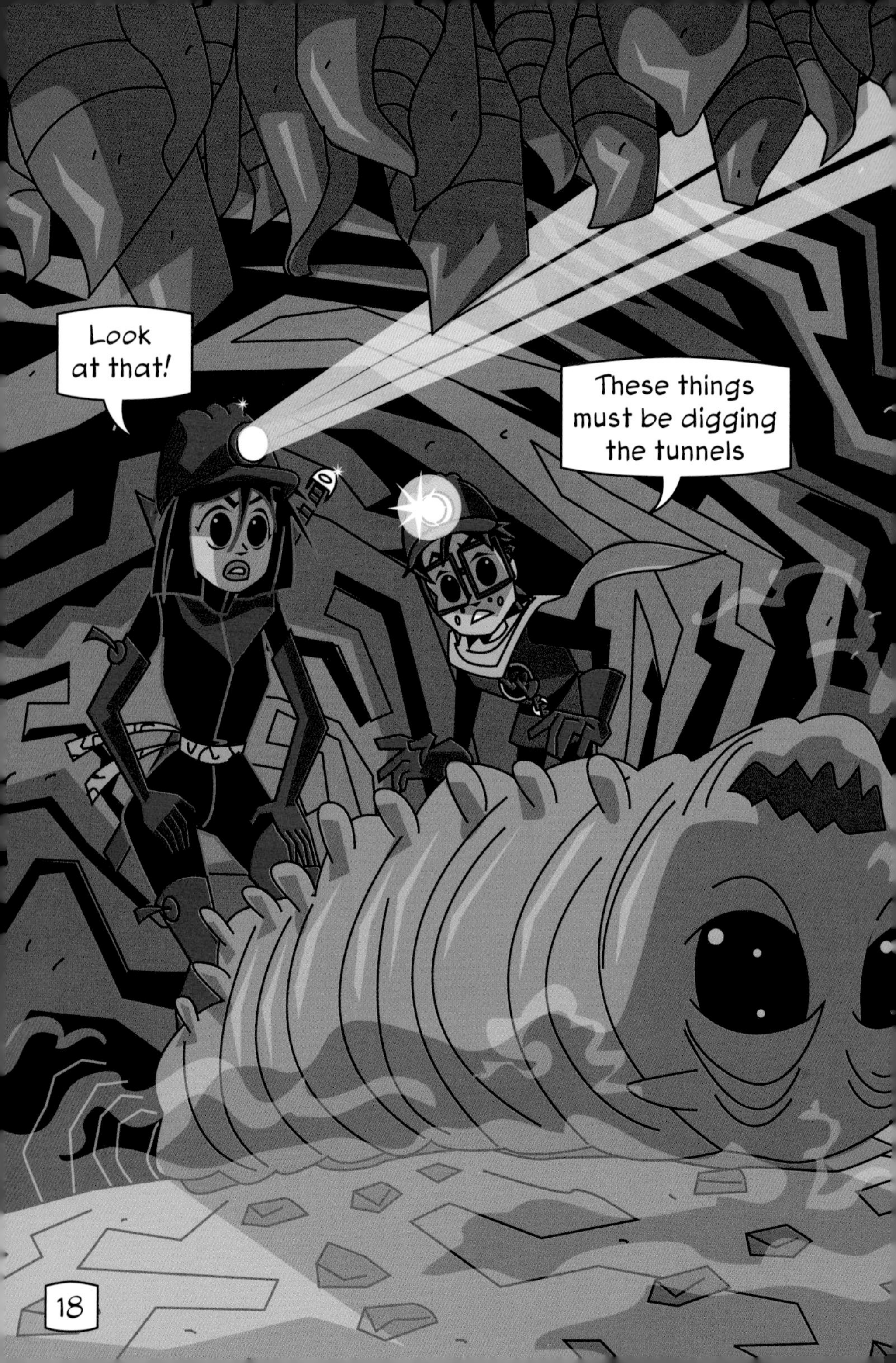
Look at that!
These things must be digging the tunnels

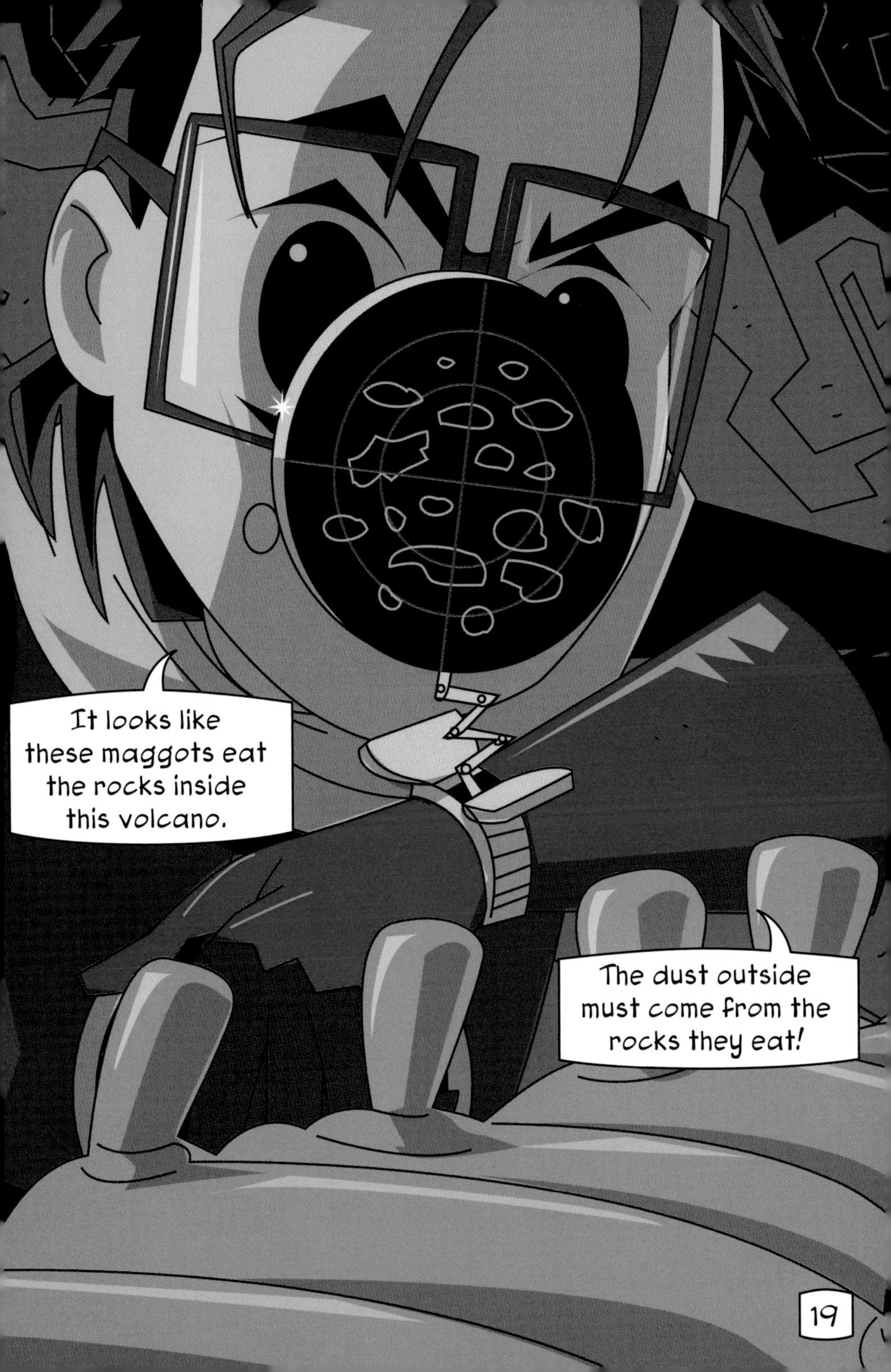
It looks like these maggots eat the rocks inside this volcano.
The dust outside must come from the rocks they eat!

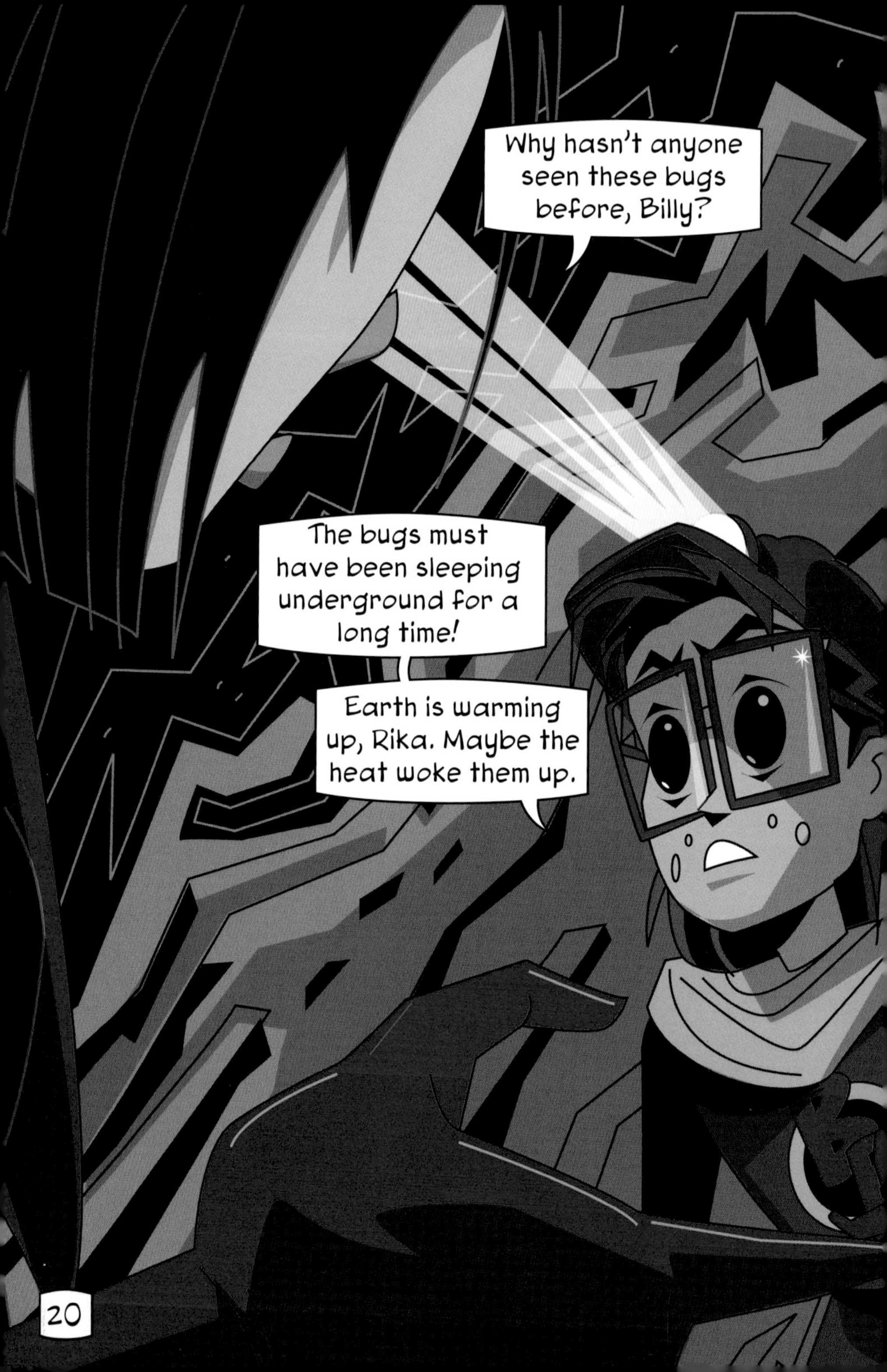
Why hasn't anyone seen these bugs before, Billy?
The bugs must have been sleeping underground for a long time!
Earth is warming up, Rika. Maybe the heat woke them up.

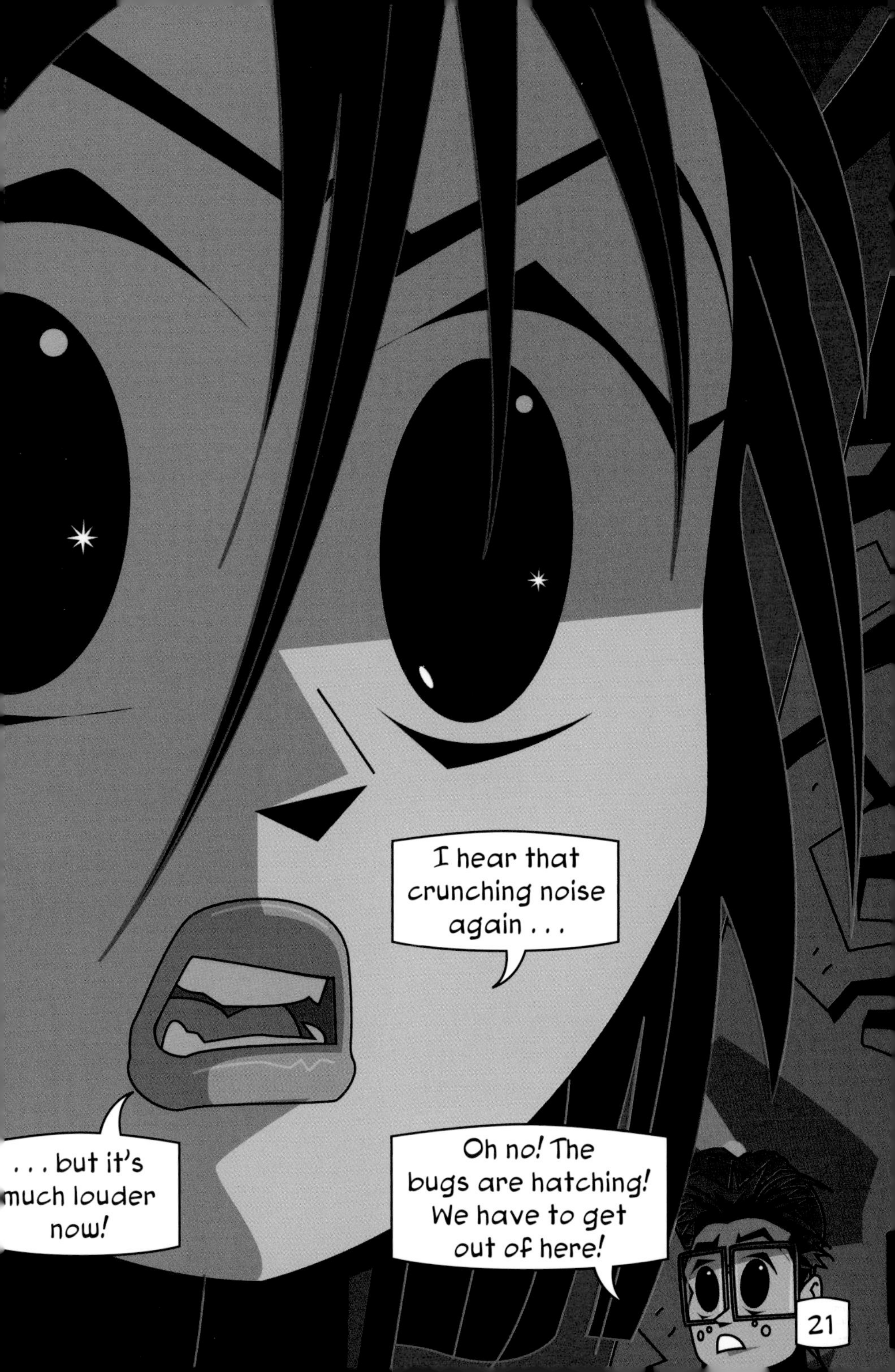
I hear that crunching noise again . . .
. . . but it's much louder now!
Oh no! The bugs are hatching! We have to get out of here!

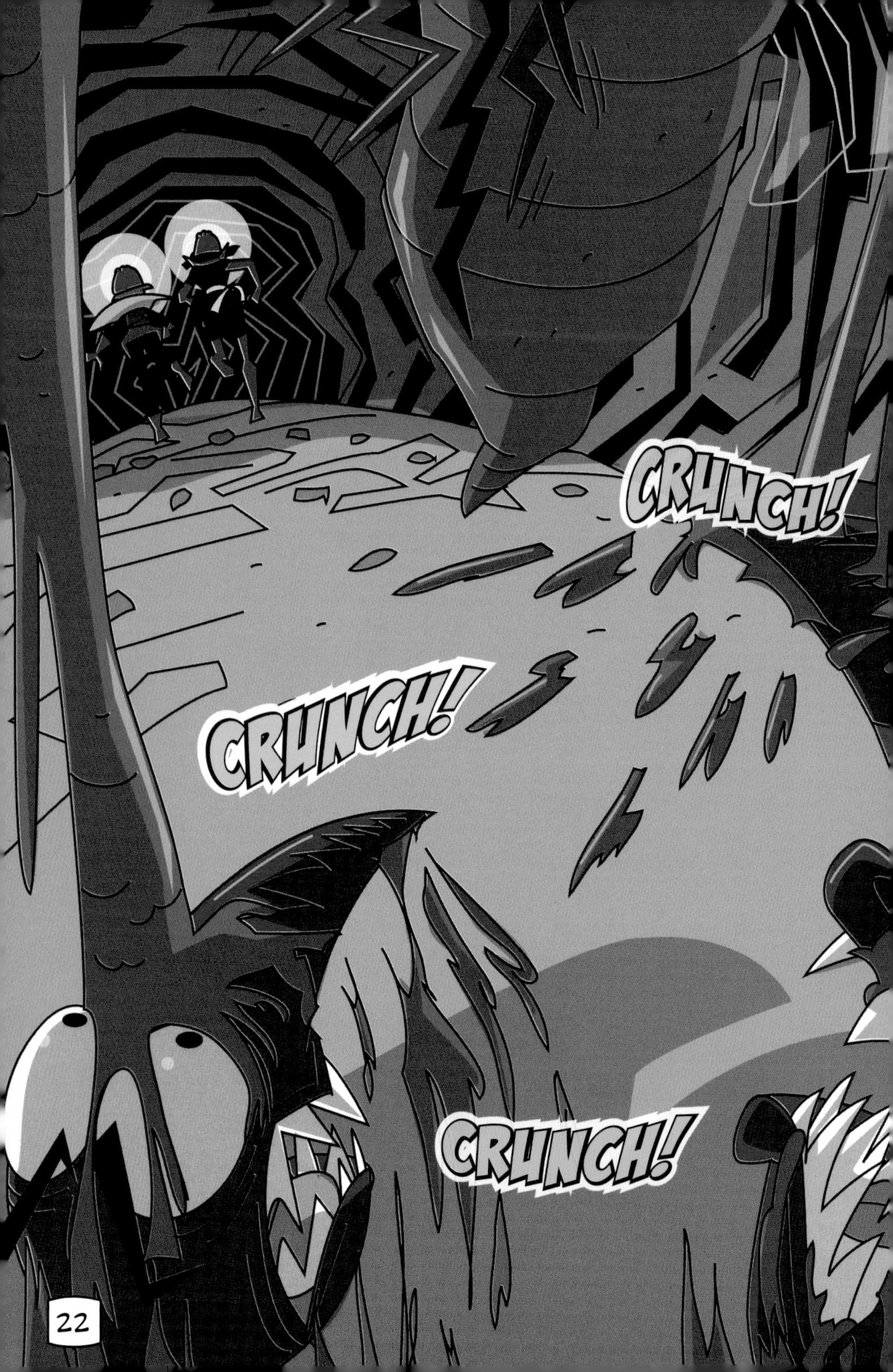
CRUNCH!
CRUNCH!
CRUNCH!

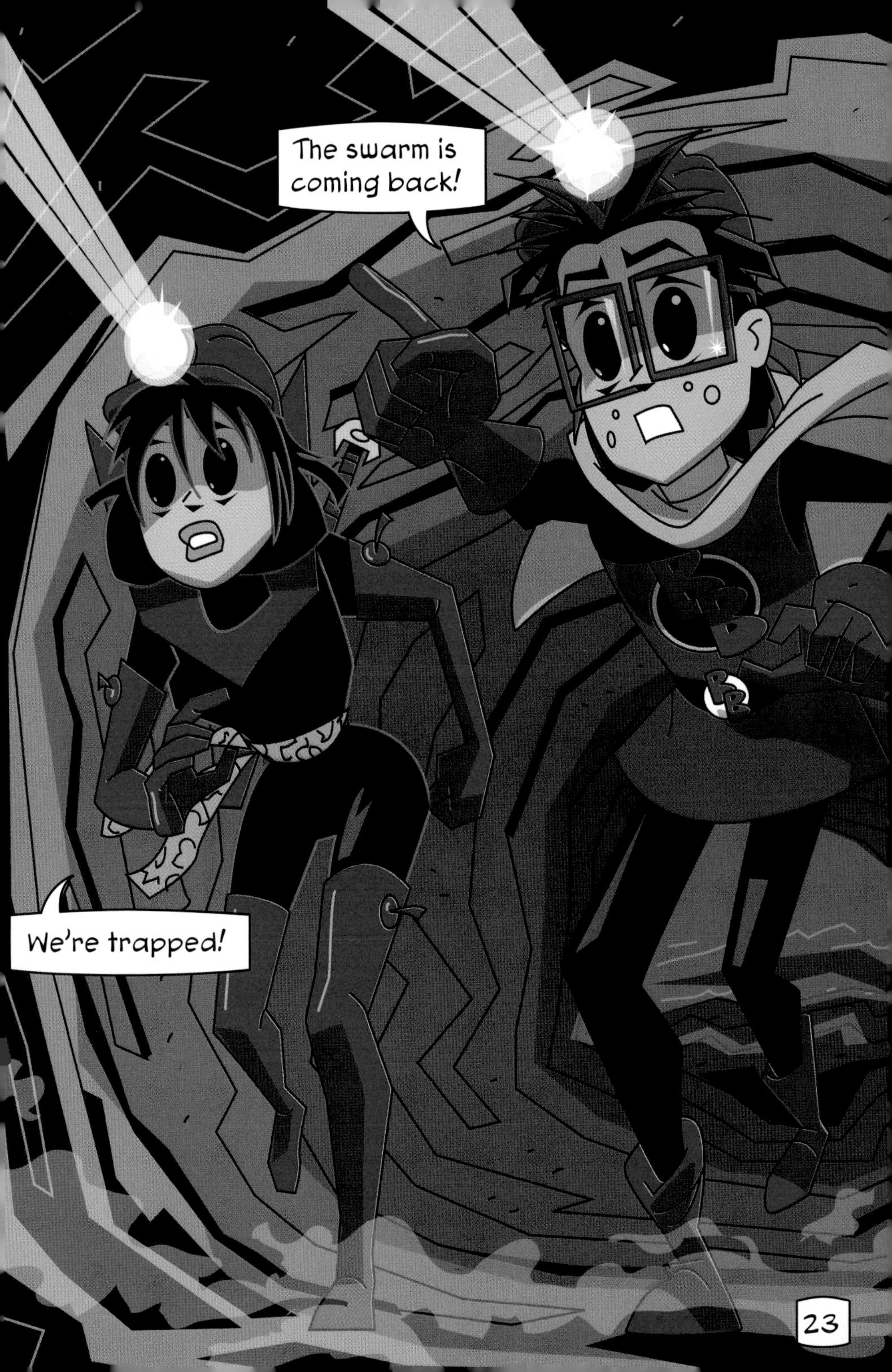
The swarm is coming back!
We're trapped!

The evil bugs catch Billy and Rika.

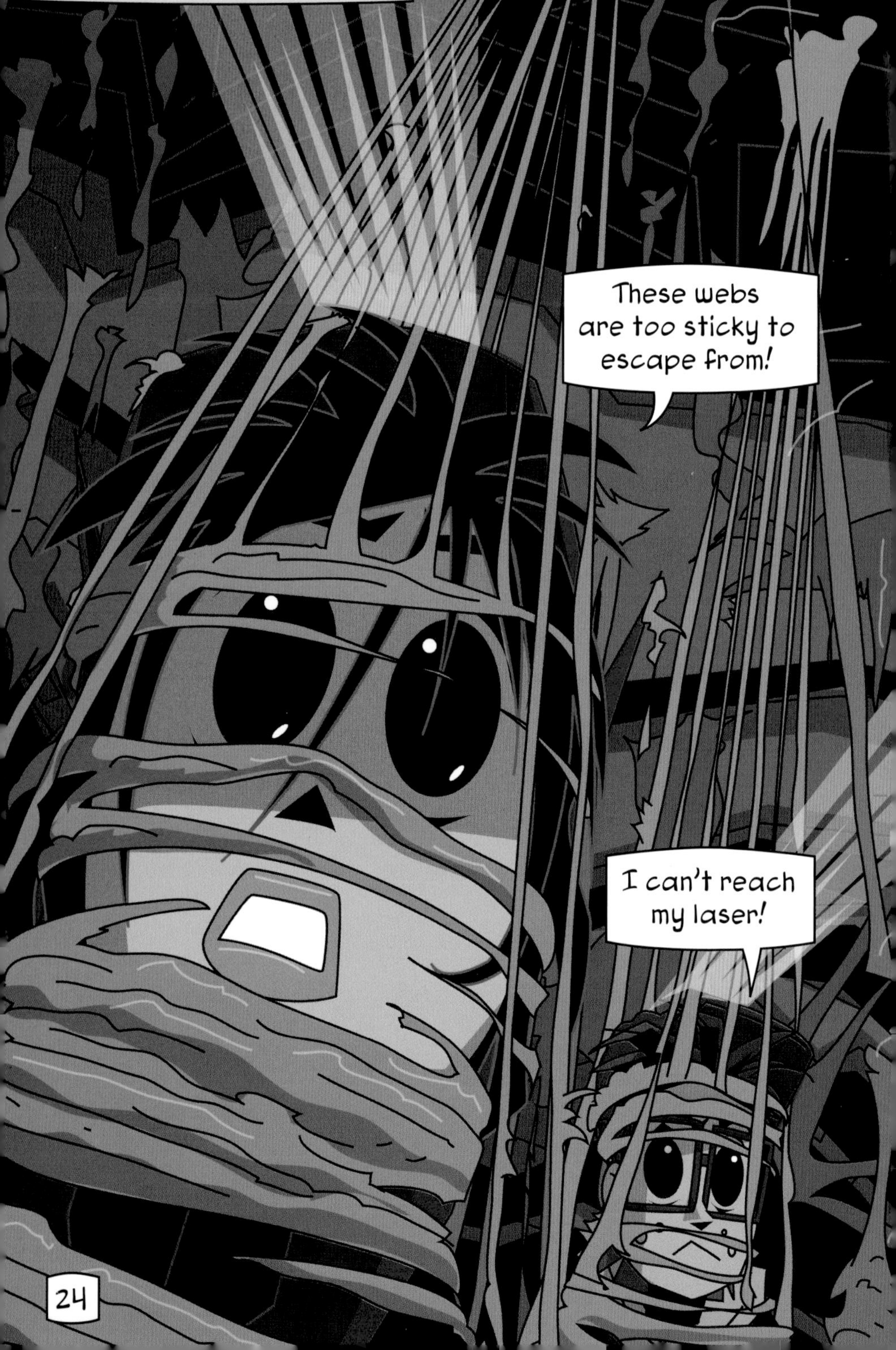
These webs are too sticky to escape from!
I can't reach my laser!

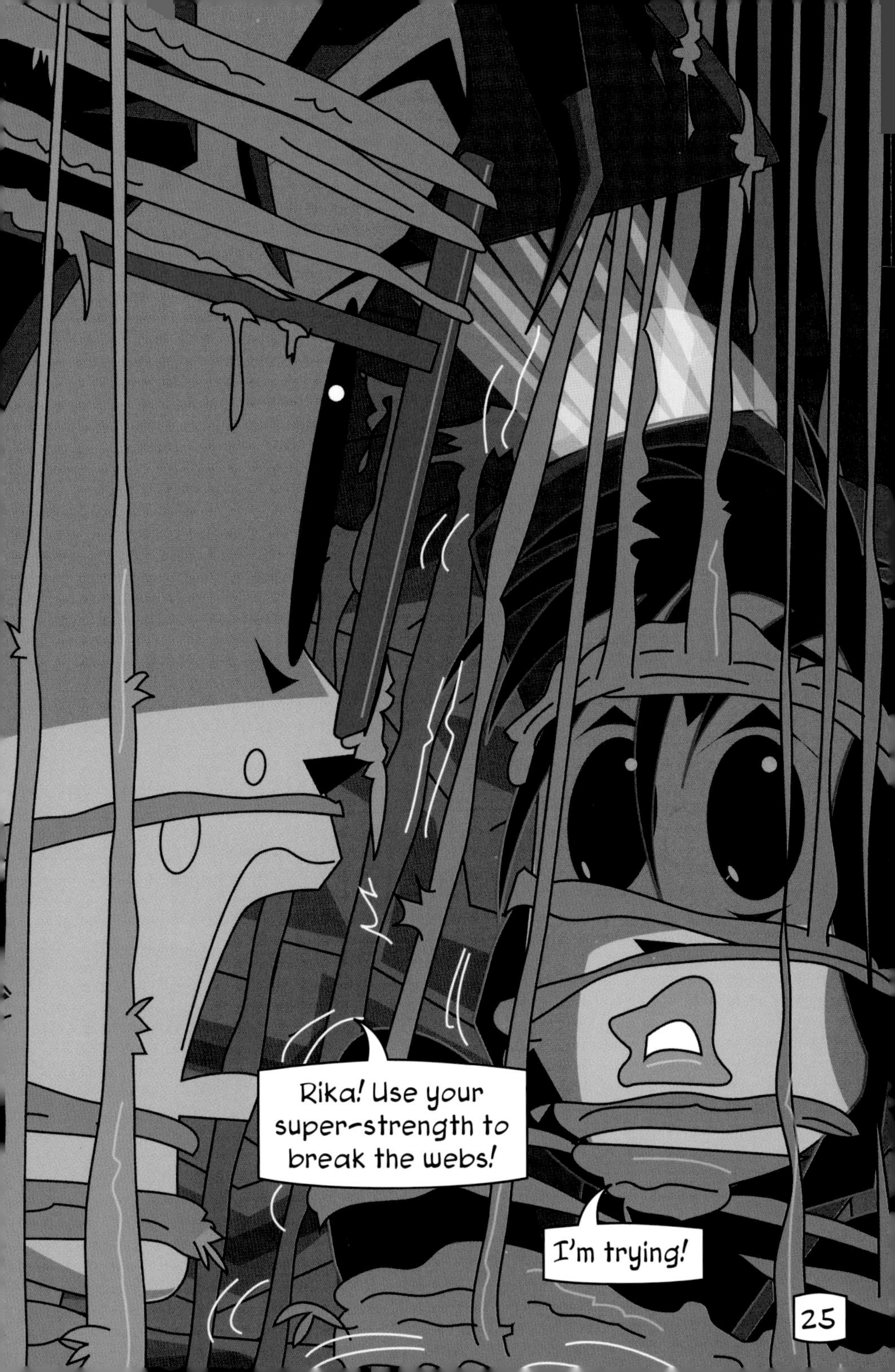
Rika! Use your super-strength to break the webs!
I'm trying!

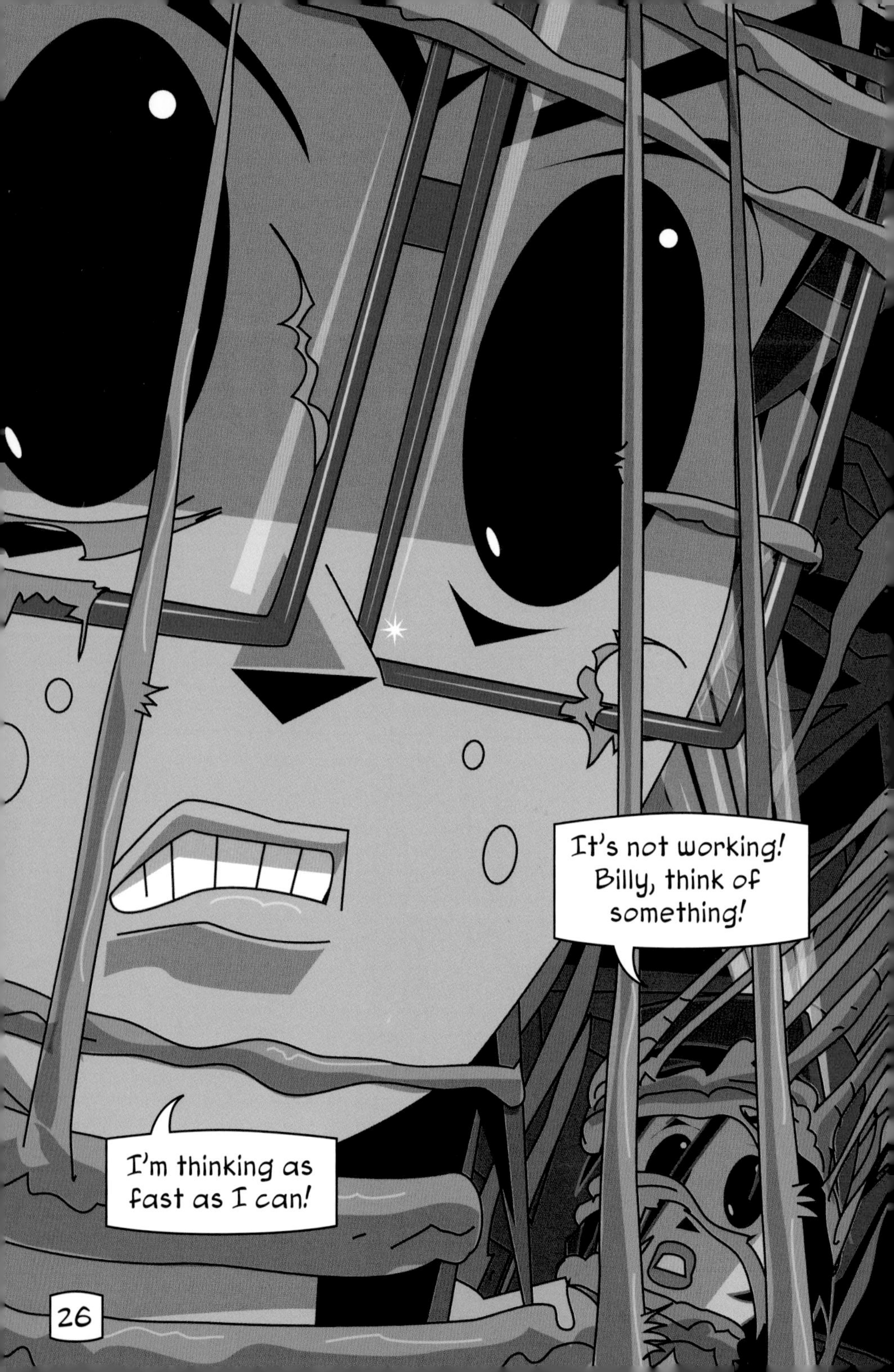
It's not working! Billy, think of something!
I'm thinking as fast as I can!

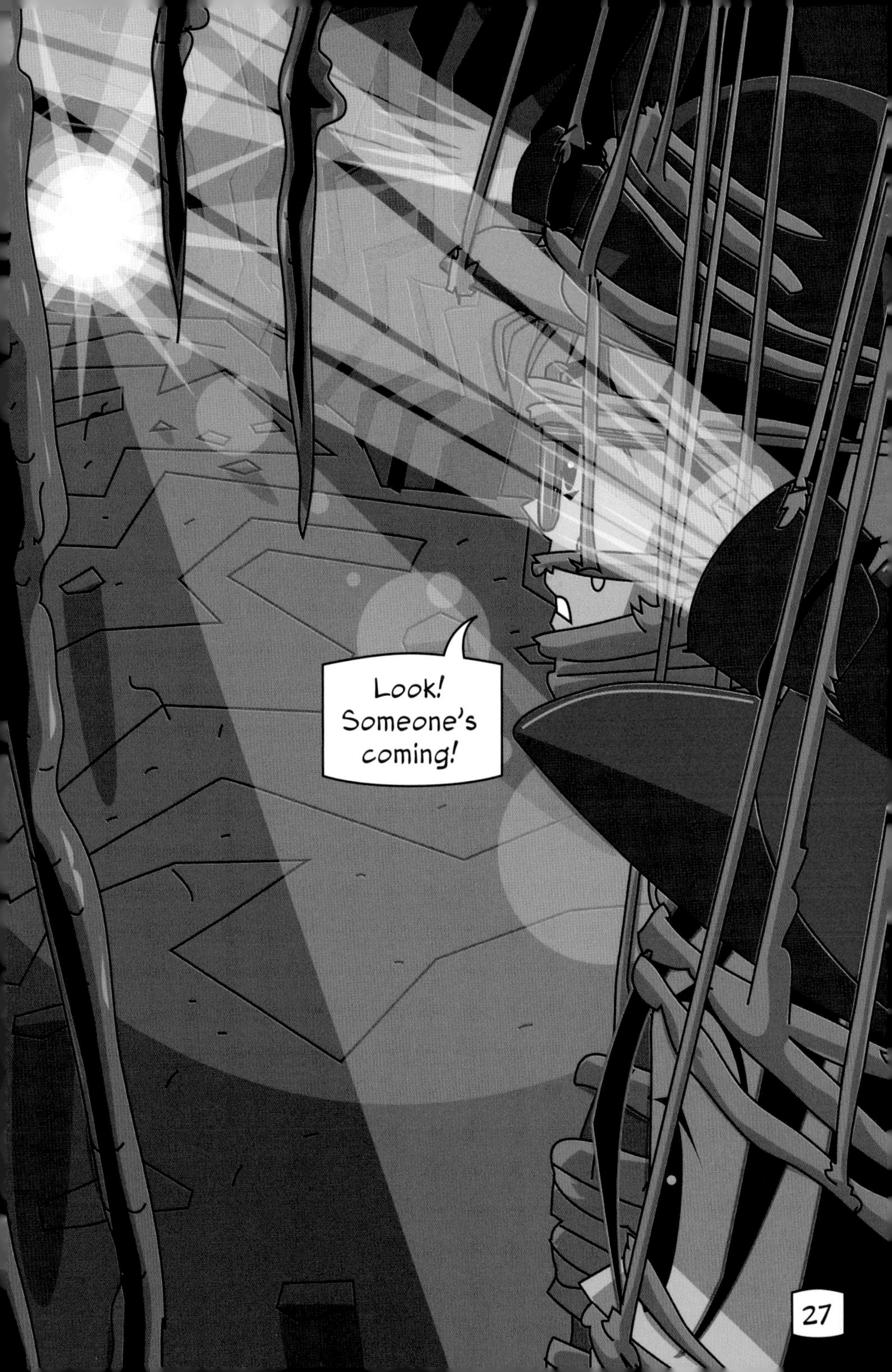
Look! Someone's coming!

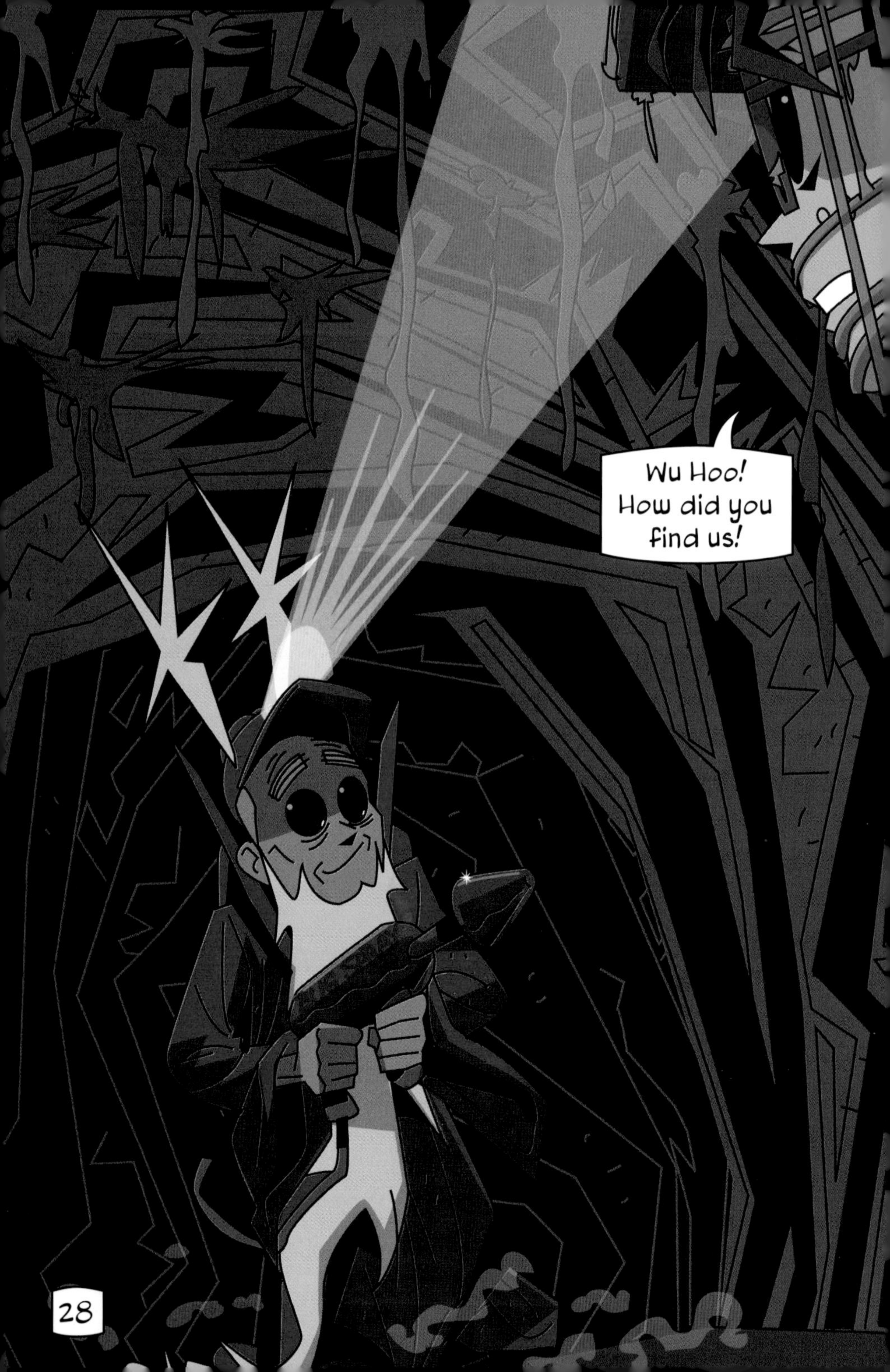
Wu Hoo!
How did you
find us!

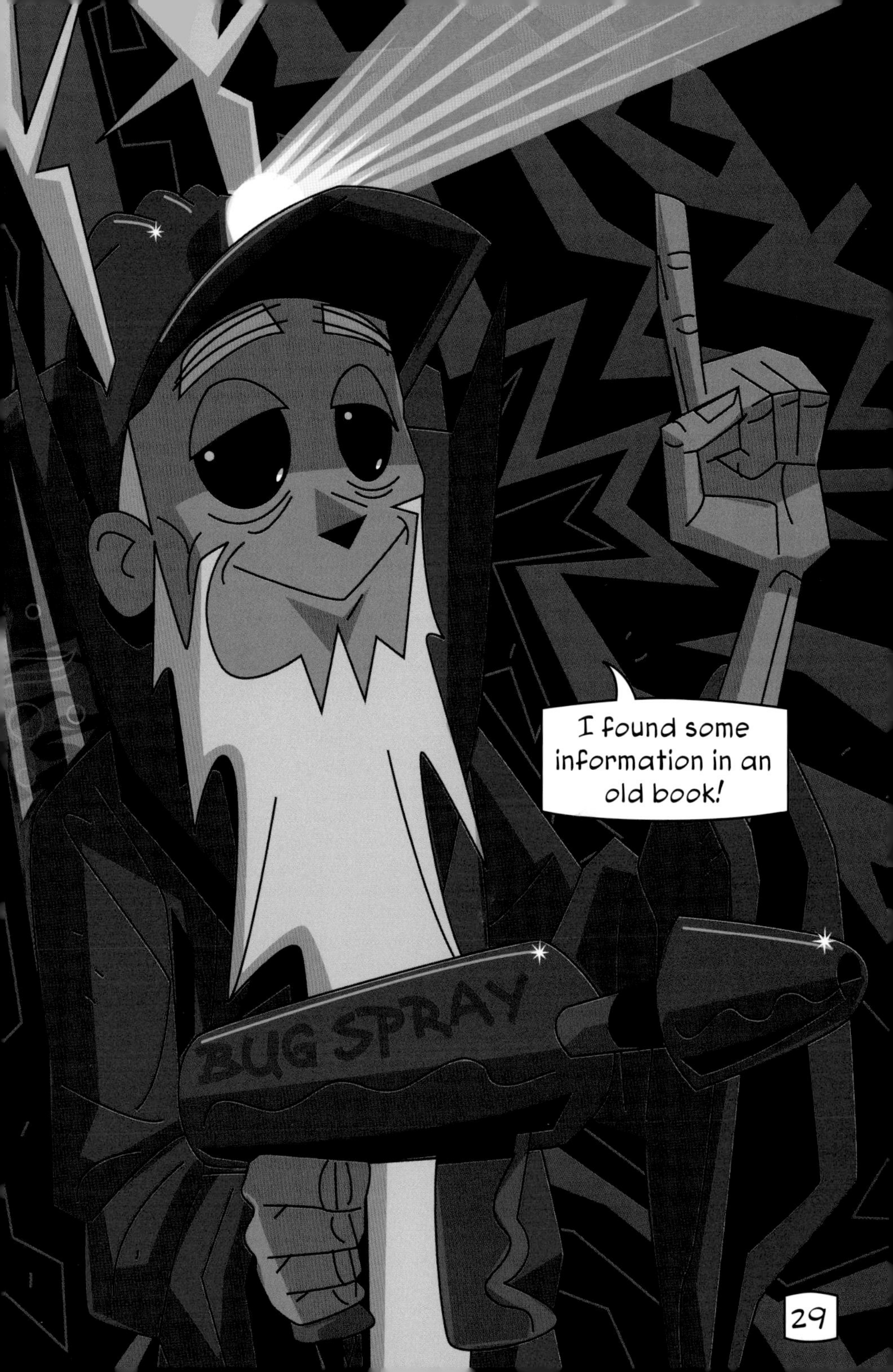
I found some information in an old book!
BUG SPRAY

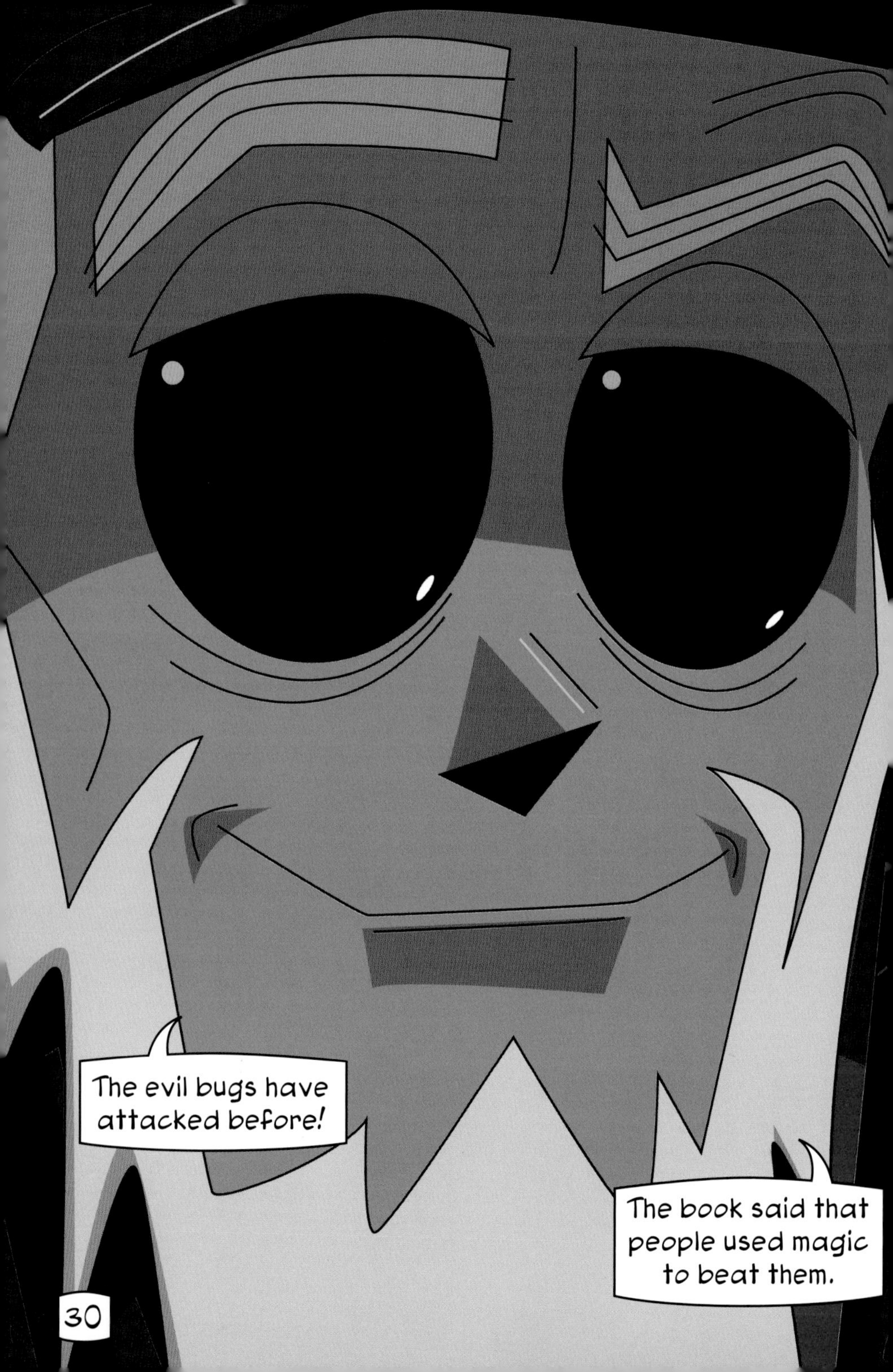
The evil bugs have attacked before!
The book said that people used magic to beat them.

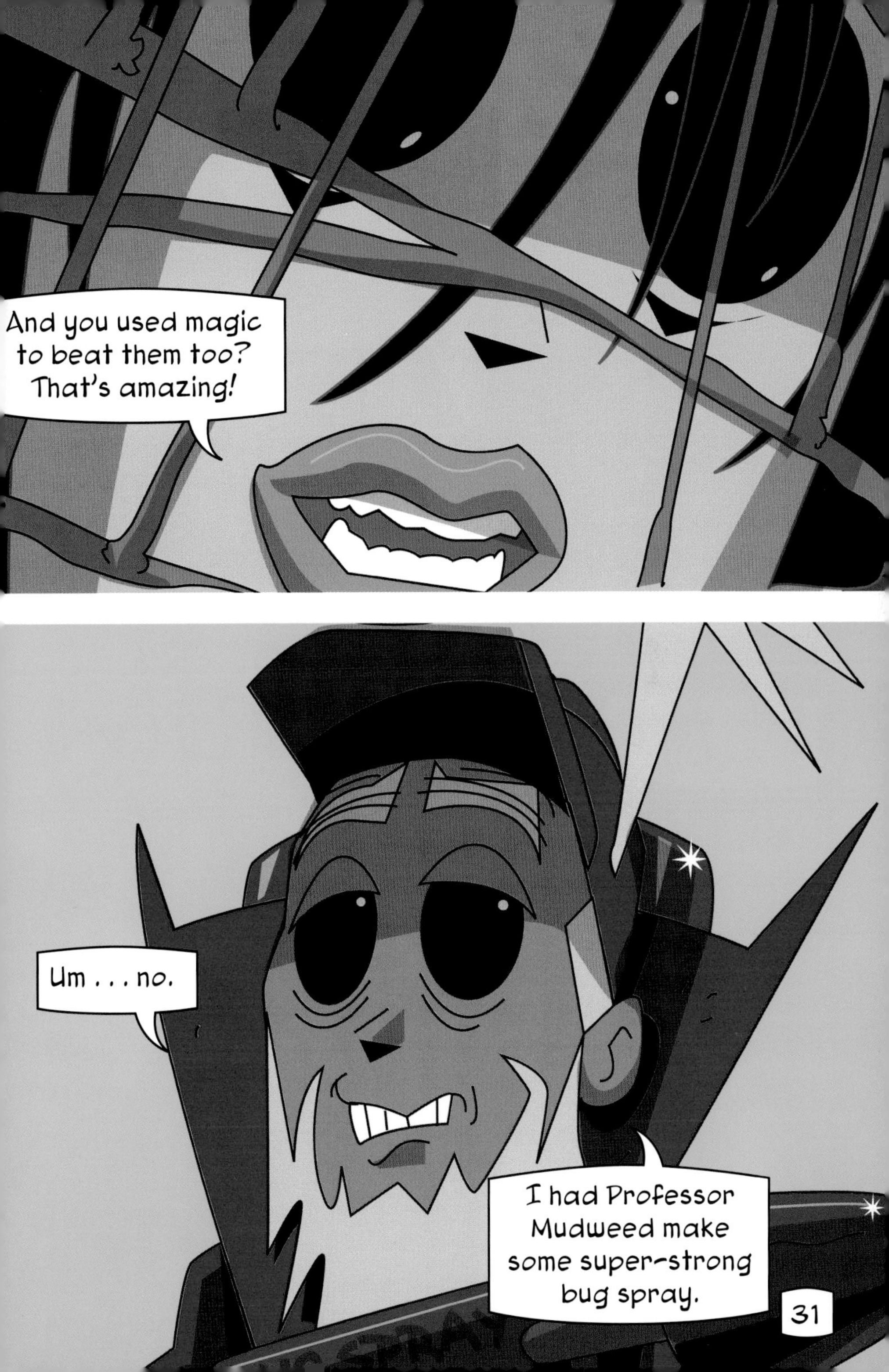
And you used magic to beat them too? That's amazing!
Um . . . no.
I had Professor Mudweed make some super-strong bug spray.

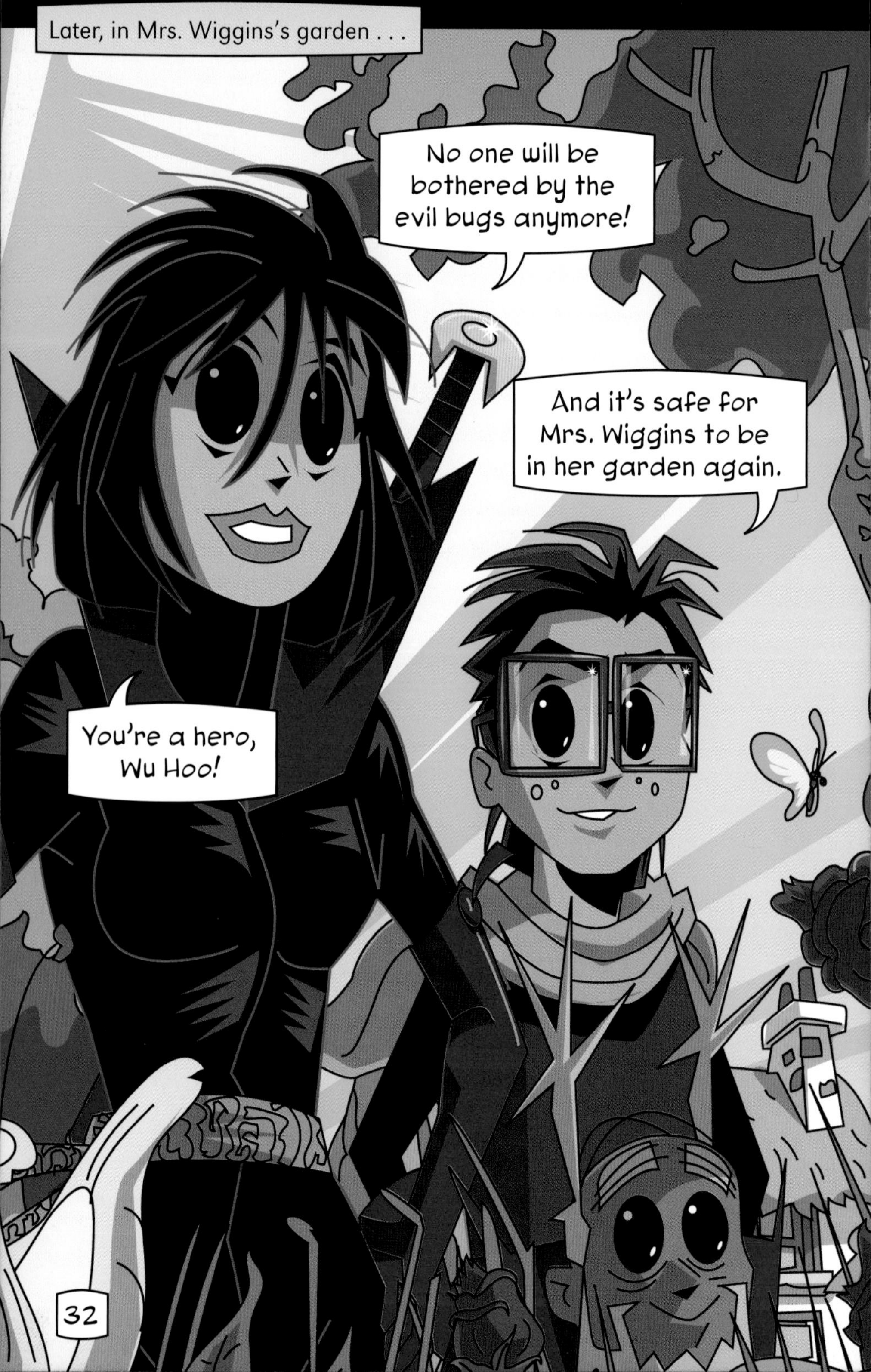

Later, in Mrs. Wiggins's garden . . .
No one will be bothered by the evil bugs anymore!
And it's safe for Mrs. Wiggins to be in her garden again.
You're a hero, Wu Hoo!